READING CORNER

PHONICS

Mr Boot's Band

Written by
Sue Graves

Illustrated by
Daniel Postgate

Practising long vowel phonemes,
CVCC and CCVC plus polysyllabic words

First published in 2010 by
Franklin Watts
338 Euston Road
London NW1 3BH

Franklin Watts Australia
Hachette Children's Books
Level 17/207 Kent Street
Sydney NSW 2000

A CIP catalogue record for this book
is available from the British Library.

ISBN: 978 0 7496 9168 4 (hbk)
ISBN: 978 0 7496 9177 6 (pbk)

Series Editor: Jackie Hamley
Series Advisors: Dr Barrie Wade,
 Dr Hilary Minns
Series Designer: Jonathan Hair

Printed in China

Franklin Watts is a division of
Hachette Children's Books,
an Hachette UK company
www.hachette.co.uk

There is a puzzle at the end of this book.
Here are the answers for you to check later!

The matching words are:
flute boot, cute, shoot
town brown, crown, gown
blew blue, dew, new
Pete beat, feet, seat

2

Mr Boot had a band.

Pete blew the cornet.

Eve blew the flute.

Mr Boot hit the big drum hard.

It was the best band in town!

11

One day, a note came
from the king.

"The king is to visit our town," said Mr Boot. "And he wants to hear our band!"

It was the day of the king's visit.

15

But Pete and Eve had bad news. They were too ill to play in the band.

16

"Oh dear!" said Mr Boot.

"What can we do?"

They all had a think.

"Got it!" Pete said. "Come on!"

The king came to town.

"Oh good!" he said. "I can hear
Mr Boot and his band."

But it was not Mr Boot and his band at all …

… it was just Mr Boot!

Mr Boot was a one man band!

He blew the cornet.

He blew the flute.

He hit the big drum hard.

"Mr Boot's one man band is the best band in the land," laughed the king.

29

Puzzle Time!

Match the words that rhyme
to the pictures.

cute

gown

dew

boot

feet

beat

blew

brown

blue

seat

shoot

Pete

crown

new

See page 2 for answers.

Notes for parents and teachers

READING CORNER PHONICS has been structured to provide maximum support for children learning to read through synthetic phonics. The stories are designed for independent reading but may also be used by adults for sharing with young children.

The teaching of early reading through synthetic phonics focuses on the 44 sounds in the English language, and how these sounds correspond to their written form in the 26 letters of the alphabet. Carefully controlled vocabulary makes these books accessible for children at different stages of phonics teaching, progressing from simple CVC (consonant-vowel-consonant) words such as "top" (t-o-p) to trisyllabic words such as "messenger" (mess-en-ger). READING CORNER PHONICS allows children to read words in context, and also provides visual clues and repetition to further support their reading. These books will help develop the all important confidence in the new reader, and encourage a love of reading that will last a lifetime!

If you are reading this book with a child, here are a few tips:

1. Talk about the story before you start reading. Look at the cover and the title. What might the story be about? Why might the child like it?

2. Encourage the child to reread the story, and to retell the story in their own words, using the illustrations to remind them what has happened.

3. Discuss the story and see if the child can relate it to their own experience, or perhaps compare it to another story they know.

4. Give praise! Small mistakes need not always be corrected. If a child is stuck on a word, ask them to try and sound it out and then blend it together again, or model this yourself. For example "wish" w-i-sh "wish".

READING CORNER PHONICS covers two grades of synthetic phonics teaching, with three levels at each grade. Each level has a certain number of words per story, indicated by the number of bars on the spine of the book:

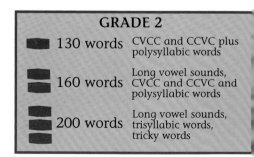

GRADE 1	
50 words	CVC words with short vowel sounds
70 words	CVC words plus sounds of more than one letter
100 words	Sounds of more than one letter, simple polysyllabic words

GRADE 2	
130 words	CVCC and CCVC plus polysyllabic words
160 words	Long vowel sounds, CVCC and CCVC and polysyllabic words
200 words	Long vowel sounds, trisyllabic words, tricky words